The
Boy
Who
Wouldn't
Share

For Xeth Feinberg and the Icebox Gang:
Howard, John, Rob, and especially Tal.
—M.R.

To my brother, Dan, who I shared my Lionel HO electric train with—
can I PLEASE have it back now?
—D.C.

THE BOY WHO WOULDN'T SHARE
Text copyright © 2008 by Mike Reiss
Illustrations copyright © 2008 by David Catrow

ISBN 978-0-06-059132-8
Designed by Stephanie Bart-Horvath

Printed at RR Donnelley

Reynosa, Tamaulipas, Mexico

December 2009

The Boy Who Wouldn't Share

By Mike Reiss

Illustrated by
David Catrow

HarperCollinsPublishers

Edward was
a frightful boy
who wouldn't share
a single toy.

Even with his sister, Claire,
Edward simply would not share.

She could not ride his rocking horse.

"IT'S MINE!" he said.
"Not yours, of course!"

She could not wear
his wizard's hat.

"IT'S MINE!" he said.
"Now give me that!"

She could not hug his teddy bear.

"IT'S MINE!" he said.
"Why should I share?"

She could not even TOUCH his Slinky.

"IT'S MINE!"
he said.

"You'll make
it stinky!"

As for his blow~up
frankenstein?

"IT'S MINE!" he said.
"IT'S MINE.
MINE.
MINE!"

Edward went into a rage
if she went near his hamster cage,
his truck,
his duck,
his train, his bike,
a doll he didn't even
really like,
his hockey stick,
his bowling ball.

"THEY'RE
MINE!"
he said.
"I
WANT
THEM
ALL!"

You could just see
Edward's little smile
from somewhere deep
inside the pile.

When Edward's mom came in with fudge,
Edward found he couldn't budge.
His mother didn't see him there,
and so she gave it all to Claire.

But Claire knew
it was only fair
to share her fudge
with Teddy Bear.

Edward knew that he'd been crabby,
grouchy, grumbly, greedy, grabby.
"Share my toys," said Edward.
"Take them.
Hold them!
Hug them!

You can break them!"

And Claire,
who did not hold a grudge,
helped him out
and gave him fudge.

"Sorry,"
said Edward.

"It's my fault.
IT'S MINE."

And wouldn't you know it?

The
day
turned
out
fine.